Text copyright © 2020 by Kyle Lukoff
Illustrations copyright © 2020 by Mark Hoffmann
Published in Canada and the USA in 2020 by Groundwood Books

Groundwood Books / House of Anansi Press
groundwoodbooks.com

The publisher would like to thank Kevin Connolly for checking the text.

We gratefully acknowledge the Government of Canada for its financial support of our publishing program.

With the participation of the Government of Canada
Avec la participation du gouvernement du Canada | Canadä

Library and Archives Canada Cataloguing in Publication
Title: Explosion at the poem factory / Kyle Lukoff ; pictures by Mark Hoffmann.
Names: Lukoff, Kyle, author. | Hoffmann, Mark, illustrator.
Identifiers: Canadiana (print) 2019014677X | Canadiana (ebook) 20190147350 | ISBN 9781773061320 (hardcover) |
ISBN 9781773061337 (EPUB) | ISBN 9781773063515 (Kindle)
Classification: LCC PZ7.1.L85 Exp 2020 | DDC 813/.6—dc23

The illustrations were created with acrylic, pastel and colored pencil.
Design by Michael Solomon
Printed and bound in Malaysia

To the Podilectern, the full Philo coat rack (currently in absentia), the clock on the wall of the Charles V. Paterno Library, and all the lifetime members of the Philolexian society. — KL

For my Montserrat College of Art family, especially Allison and Alyssa. — MH

EXPLOSION AT THE POEM FACTORY

KYLE LUKOFF

PICTURES BY

MARK HOFFMANN

GROUNDWOOD BOOKS

HOUSE OF ANANSI PRESS

TORONTO   BERKELEY

When automatic pianos came to Luddston, Kilmer Watts had to find a new job. He had spent years teaching people the intricacies of fingering, the ins and outs of sonatas, and the importance of heart and soul.

But with these newfangled machines you could push a button and the piano would do the playing for you — five times the sound without a second wasted on practice.

Kilmer didn't know what else he was good at but had always wondered what went on inside the poem factory.

Weren't poems made by hand?

"That's horse-and-buggy talk!" boomed the foreman. "Back in my day we had to wait weeks, months even, for creaky old bards to deliver the goods. Our modern world needs assembly-line poetics, don't you think? New poems for a new day! Why spend hours wrestling with rhymes when our prosodizer can find the perfect synonym with the flip of a switch?"

9

Kilmer looked around at the buzzing, clanking machines. Maybe the foreman was right. And he needed a job.

Soon Kilmer learned how to operate the meter meter and empty the cliché bins. The voltatron stopped making him nervous, and the amphibracher wasn't as complicated as it looked.

It was easy to assemble a poem. Pick a rhyme scheme, sprinkle in some similes, don't overdo the refrains, always add alliteration.

The multipurpose poem industry was booming, and the factory shipped everything from odes to epithalamiums to markets across the land.

Kilmer made mistakes, of course. A poem rhyming "box" with "talk" resulted in hundreds of angry letters. A hiccup in the scansion scanner resulted in a batch of haiku with two, four, even five times the acceptable number of syllables. Several sheets of blank verse came out entirely blank.

After that he made sure to keep a close eye on the details, and life was sweet.

But one morning, when Kilmer had been working at the poem factory for a year and a day, disaster struck.

First, the metaphor unmixer malfunctioned. There was a clog in the drainage pipe, and mixed metaphors threatened to overflow the vat. The assembly line began to self-deconstruct, and the machine failures cascaded catastrophically.

Rhymes wrenched. The spring sprang
out of the sprung rhythm. The amphibracher
broke. The enjambment jammed. The anacrusis
encrusted. And the kenning ceased to ken.

Kilmer was at his trusty old meter meter
and noticed the assembly line moving as slow as
molossus. The machines began to make the most
terrible onomatopoeias, and the ceiling started
to shake.

Kilmer scanned the factory in a panic. He knew something was terribly wrong but didn't know how to fix it. He tried to warn his fellow poemsmiths.

"Get out! Get out!" Kilmer shouted.
"Before the building falls! The stress!
The stress! It's tearing down the walls!"

The screeching, banging, crashing, clanging of the cacophonous factory was overwhelming. No one could hear his heroic couplet, but clearly something was a-foot.

The workers piled onto delivery trochees or galloped as fast as their feet could carry them, escaping just beats before the factory's structural concrete verses shattered and lay splintered acrostic the shop floor.

When he had recovered from the trauma, Kilmer needed a job again. And the people of Luddston and beyond still needed their poems. He went back to giving lessons, this time teaching people the difference between a sonnet and a sestina, and when to use a caesura.

There were fewer poems than before. Plenty of Kilmer's students overused hyperbole and empty clichés. Far too many forced through an uncomfortable rhyme scheme. But even the simplest stanza had within it a beating heart.

Since nobody had to practice the piano and everyone wanted to share their poems, Kilmer took it upon himself to organize a reading. The Lays of Luddston, he called it. Towns that had previously relied upon imported verse came to listen, and left with their own ideas.

The poem industry may have suffered, but poetry would survive.

Assembled Lines

Explosion at the Poem Factory can be fun to read even if you don't know the difference between an anapest and an enjambment. But if you're curious about what all of these uncommon words mean, I hope these definitions help!

FEET

A "foot" is the building block of a poem. Every two-, three- and four-syllable word and phrase is a type of foot.

You know how the words "desert" and "dessert" sound very similar, even though they mean different things? (As I'm sure you know, a DES-ert is a dry and sandy place, while a dess-ERT is a sweet end to dinner.) The two words sound different because you put the emphasis, or stress, on a different syllable in each of these two-syllable words. If we wanted to describe desert and dessert in feet, we would say that desert is a "trochee," while dessert is an "iamb."

When feet are organized into a pattern, they can become a specific kind of poem.

Here are some examples of some feet (but not every possible foot):

Amphibrach: A three-syllable foot where the stress is on the middle syllable (like the word "em-BARR-ass").

Anapest: A three-syllable foot where the stress is on the last syllable (like the phrase "Time to GO!").

Dactyl: A three-syllable foot where the stress is on the first syllable (like the word "BI-cycle").

Iamb: A two-syllable foot where the stress is on the second syllable (like the word "be-LOW").

Molossus: A three-syllable foot where all three syllables are stressed. (I'm not sure if these actually exist.)

Trochee: A two-syllable foot where the stress is on the first syllable (like the word "DOUGH-nut").

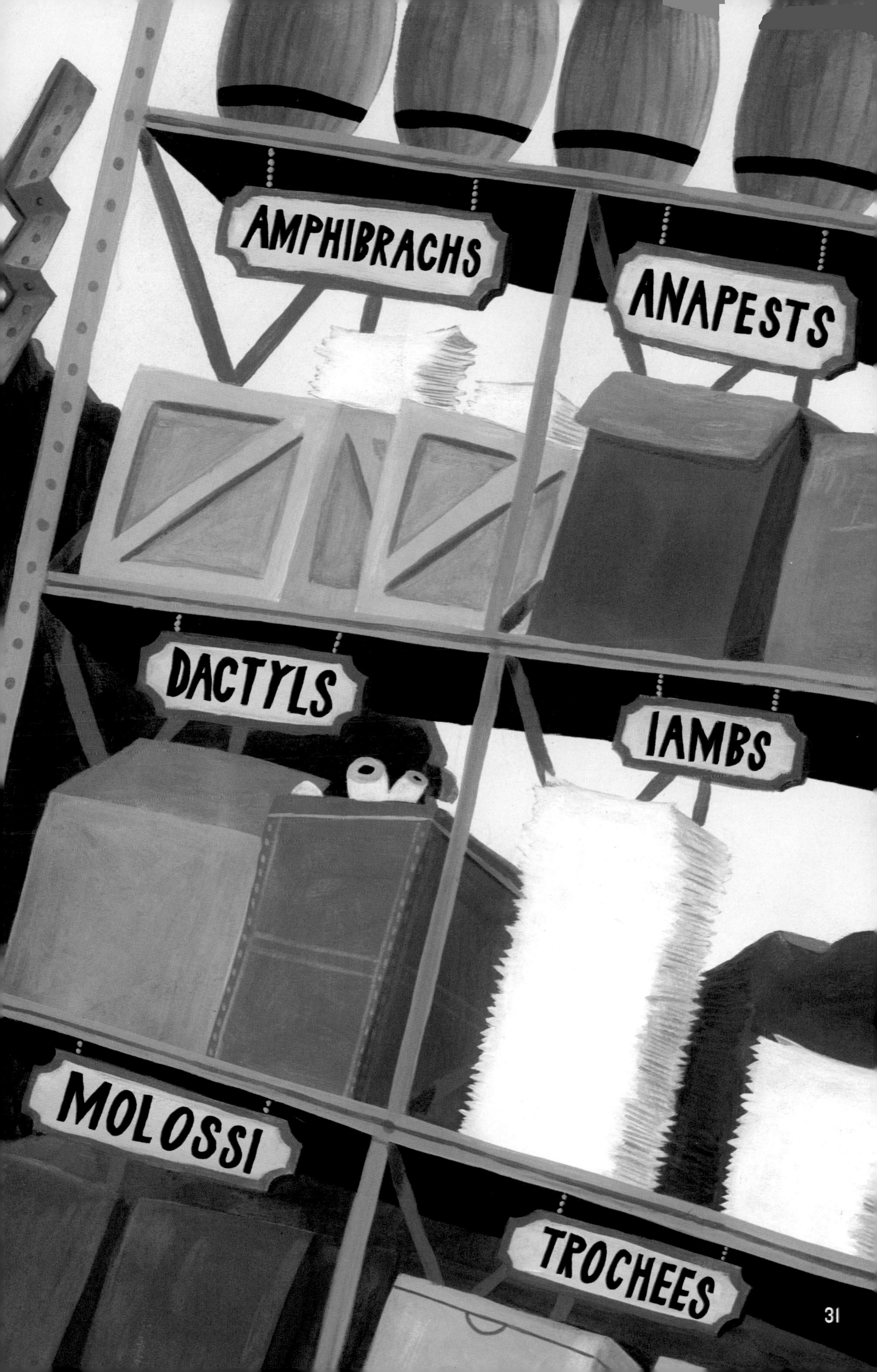
AMPHIBRACHS
ANAPESTS
DACTYLS
IAMBS
MOLOSSI
TROCHEES

SOME TYPES OF POEMS

Acrostic: When a certain letter in each line of a poem spells out a word. An acrostic for the name Kyle could be

Kicks
Yellow
Lemons
Everywhere.

Concrete verse: A poem where the words on the page are arranged into a picture that represents the poem's subject or meaning.

HERE, EVERYTHING IS GRAY AND FLAT.
ON THE OTHER SIDE IS SOMEWHERE ELSE,
BOUNDED BY A POT OF GOLD ON EITHER END.
I KNOW THAT SOMEDAY I WILL LEAVE THIS PLACE
AND FIND THE JOYS THAT OTHER LANDS CAN HOLD.
UNTIL THEN I WILL MAKE THE LIGHT MYSELF.

Epithalamium: A poem that celebrates a marriage.

Haiku: A traditional form of Japanese poetry with strict rules about length and subject. Haiku are usually about nature and try to express a feeling by describing a moment or setting. They can also be written in English and typically have a specific number of syllables per line — five in the first line, seven in the second and five in the third. Here is my example of a haiku:

> Not the first snowfall;
> Ground freezes reluctantly,
> Branches bend and sigh.

Heroic couplet: Two rhyming lines, five iambs in each ten-syllable line (called "iambic pentameter"). Kilmer shouts a heroic couplet when he realizes the factory is going to explode.

Lay: A poem that tells a story, usually a story of adventure or romance.

Ode: An ancient form of poetry that is usually dedicated to someone or something.

Sestina: A very complicated kind of poem. It has six stanzas of six lines each. The last words of the first six lines repeat as the last words of every line in each stanza, in a specific order. The last stanza, called an "envoi," must be three lines, and uses those six end words in a different pattern. Here is my example of a sestina (see if you can figure out the pattern of the end words!):

PRINCESS: A SESTINA

Emily decided to become a princess.
According to the movies, it was a lot of fun.
Everything in your closet could be pink,
And you never had to share your toys.
No matter what game you chose, your friends couldn't argue,
And princesses never had to work.

She gathered up her playthings and went to work.
But they weren't sure if they wanted a princess.
Emily refused to argue.
"Being a royal subject," she promised everyone, "will be a lot of fun."
She began making decrees to her toys
In her favorite dress, which of course was pink.

Her teddy bear did not want to wear pink.
The dump truck just wanted to read, not work.
Emily didn't realize there would be opinions amongst her toys.
But commanding royal subjects was part of being a princess.
Bossing them around was great fun
Until her subjects began to argue.

"I'm the real princess here! Don't argue!"
Cried the doll in a gown that was pinker than pink.
Her bouncy ball whined, "I just want to have some fun."
The truck and bear refused to work.
Emily crossed her arms and adjusted her crown. "I am your princess!
What kind of ruler listens to mere toys?"

Her jump rope said, "You would be miserable without your toys."
Emily turned her back on it. She wouldn't — couldn't — argue.
Being a kid had been more fun than being a princess.
Tears brimmed in her eyes. Her cheeks turned pink.
"Please don't be mad! I guess this didn't work."
Turns out that being a princess wasn't even a little fun.

Playing together was a lot more fun
Than trying to boss around her toys.
It was also a whole lot less work,
And there were no more — well, fewer — reasons to argue.
Her crayons helped her make a sign, in orange and green and purple and pink.

We all play together here.
No one is the princess.

The toys would still sometimes argue,
But Emily sat on her pink rug and together they would work
It out. Being their friend was more fun than being their princess.

Sonnet: Another complicated kind of poem (but maybe less complicated than a sestina). There are a few different kinds of sonnets, but most sonnets are in iambic pentameter (five iambs per line) with a particular rhyme scheme. They usually end in a rhyming couplet. I wrote this example of a sonnet:

There is so much to learn at school today.
My backpack's on, my shoes are laced up tight.
I cannot stay at home and only play —
I have to learn to spell and add and write.
My teacher isn't very nice this year,
And recess feels so short that I could cry.
There is no time for library this year,
And homework piles up towards the sky.
But grown-ups just don't seem to understand
That learning only starts when school is done.
How many bugs can fit into my hand?
How do you climb a tree into the sun?
  In class we wait, and watch the world outside
  And want to grow; until then, time we'll bide.

GLOSSARY (EVEN MORE TERMS)

Alliteration: When words intentionally begin with the same sound or letter (they can be fun, but don't do them to death).

Anacrusis: An unstressed syllable sometimes placed at the beginning of a line.

Bard: A professional poet. This used to be an important job in some European countries hundreds of years ago.

Blank verse: Iambic pentameter that doesn't rhyme. The poet and playwright Shakespeare wrote many plays using blank verse.

Caesura: A pause in a line of poetry, sometimes written down || like this.

Cliché: An idea or phrase that's been used so many times that it's not interesting or meaningful anymore.

Couplet: Two rhyming lines of poetry that usually have the same meter, such as:

> You can still be a poet
> Even if you don't know it.

Enjambment: When a full sentence
is broken up
into separate
lines.
The poet William Carlos Williams wrote a lot
of poems
like this.

Hyperbole: When you exaggerate to make a point — like saying that your dad makes the best chocolate chip cookies in the entire universe (there are a lot of chocolate chip cookie recipes in the universe — have you tried all of them?).

Kenning: A two-word description for something, which can be used instead of referring to it by name — for example, using "night-gleams" for stars, or "mouth-bones" for teeth. Kennings are used a lot in poetry and stories from Scandinavia.

Luddite: A person who believes that new technology isn't always the best solution to a problem. "Luddites" originally referred to a group of people in England about two hundred years ago who tried to destroy weaving machines in their town. Now the word is usually an insult for someone who doesn't understand how the newest phone or tablet works, but being a Luddite isn't necessarily a bad thing.

Metaphor: When a writer tries to describe one thing by making you think about something else. When this story uses the metaphor "the simplest stanza had within it a beating heart," what is that saying about poetry? What does that say about hearts? Metaphors help make writing interesting and complicated, and also encourage readers to come up with their own ideas about what the author is talking about.

Meter: Another word for the rhythm of a poem.

Onomatopoeia: A word that sounds just like the sound it's describing, like "buzz" or "clank."

Prosody: The study of how a poem is built, looking at the meter, rhythm, rhyme and types of stanzas.

Refrain: A line in a poem that repeats, often at the end of each stanza.

Rhyme scheme: How the rhyming words in a poem are organized. When referring to a rhyme scheme, you use letters of the alphabet to show which lines rhyme with each other. The rhyme scheme for the sonnet on page 38 is ABABCDCDEFEFGG.

Scan: How well a poem flows when you read it out loud.

Scansion: Studying the meter of a poem, usually by making marks above the stresses in each line.

Simile: A comparison that helps you understand something better. You could say that a book is like a doorway into someone else's life, or that a poem is like putting a feeling onto paper. Similes and metaphors are very similar, but usually a simile includes the word "like" or "as," and metaphors don't.

Sprung rhythm: A kind of meter invented by the poet Gerard Manley Hopkins. Poems in sprung rhythm usually start off with a stressed syllable (so they're not iambic) and are meant to sound more like the way people normally talk.

Stanza: A group of lines that makes up part of a poem, similar to a paragraph in an essay or a story.

Strophe: A specific section, or stanza, of a poem.

Synonym: A word that means something similar to another word but isn't exactly the same. For example, "joyful," "pleased" and "content" are synonyms for "happy."

Verse: Can refer to one line or stanza of a poem, or the idea of poetry as a whole (as opposed to "prose," which refers to creative writing that isn't poetry).

Volta: From the Italian word for "turn." The volta marks the moment in a poem where it changes from one idea or feeling to another. It's an important part of a sonnet, but other kinds of poems don't have to have a volta.

Wrenched rhyme: A line of poetry that won't scan unless you put the stress on the wrong syllable of a word:

> If you want to get stuck in a bog
> Go there and play a game of leapfrog

Author's Note

This book would not exist without the Philolexian
Society of Columbia University, one of the best parts
of my college years. Philo is a debate team and literary
society with a long and illustrious history, and one of
our most popular events is the Alfred Joyce Kilmer
Memorial Bad Poetry Contest.

Kilmer was a poet and a member of Philo way back
in 1908. He is most famous for a poem called "Trees."
You might have heard it, or a poem trying to sound like
it. The first two lines are "I think that I shall never see
/ A poem lovely as a tree." He thought it was a good
poem, but he also thought it was fun to write bad poems
on purpose. Kilmer published some of these bad poems
using the name Alfred Watts.

Every year, Philos gather to honor Kilmer and read
our own intentionally bad poems. In 2007, my friend
Amitai "Schmonz" Schleier read something called
"Explosion at the Poem Factory" and won first place.

Almost ten years later, I got the idea to turn that "bad"
poem into a fun book. What you've just read is very
different from Mr. Schleier's original poem, but I thank
and commend him for letting me use the title, some
selected lines and the inspiration. *Surgam!*